JOHN PRATER

ALONG CAME TOM

THE BODLEY HEAD
LONDON

All was quiet in the house,

until Tom woke up.

We had breakfast together.

After breakfast we played at dressing-up

. . . but then along came Tom.

Mum wanted to take our photo

. . . but along came Tom.

Click!

It was a lovely day so we played
in the garden.

Then we built a den

. . . but along came Tom.

After lunch we did some drawing

. . . and so did Tom.

Then we gave the toys a party.

We got out a very difficult jigsaw.

We'd nearly finished it

. . . when along came Tom.

So we tried to watch TV

. . . with Tom.

After tea we helped to clear up.

Tom wasn't much help though.

Then came the best part of the whole day.

"Come along Tom, it's time for bed."

"Goodnight Tom."